90710 000 469 175

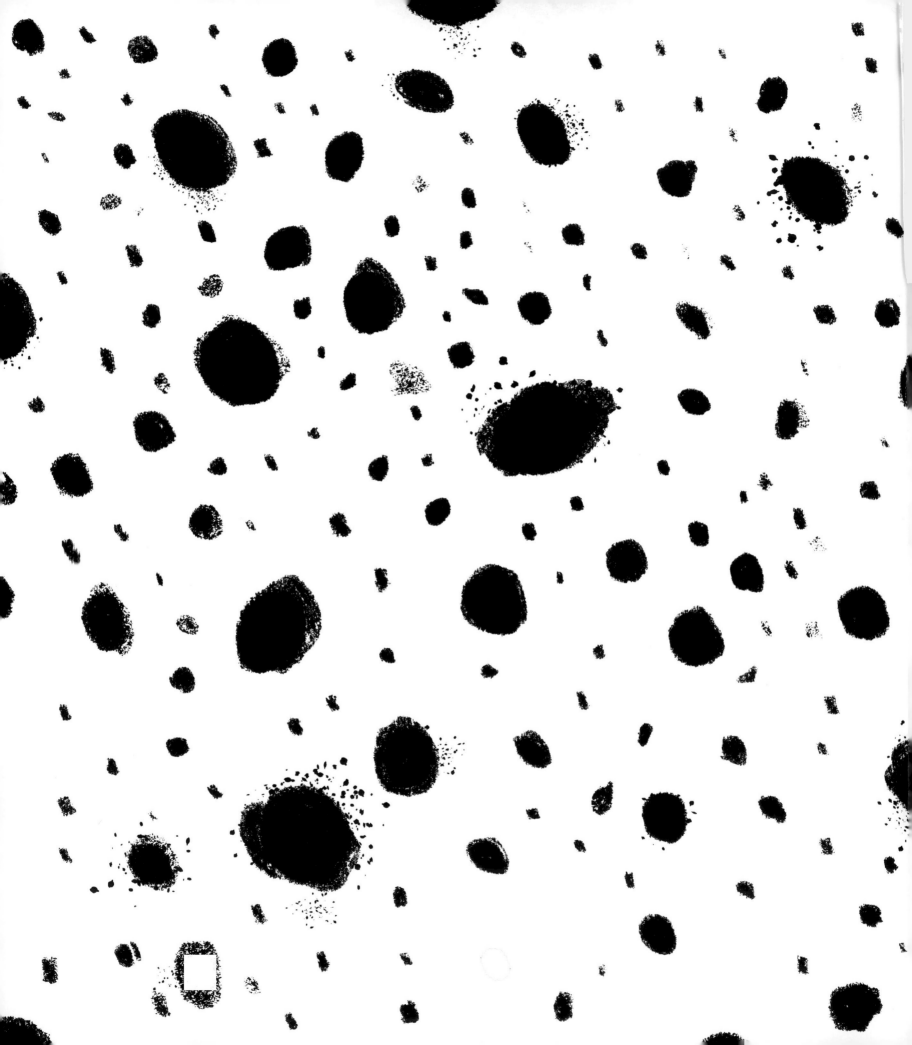

For Carys – L.H.

For Nana and Grandad – C.J.

Farshore

First published in Great Britain 2021 by Farshore
An imprint of HarperCollins*Publishers*
1 London Bridge Street, London SE1 9GF
www.farshorebooks.com

HarperCollins*Publishers*
1st Floor, Watermarque Building, Ringsend Road
Dublin 4, Ireland

Text copyright © Leigh Hodgkinson 2021
Illustrations copyright © Chris Jevons 2021

Leigh Hodgkinson and Chris Jevons have asserted their moral rights.

ISBN 978 1 4052 9820 9
Printed in the UK.
2

A CIP catalogue record for this title is available from the British Library.

ONESIE PARTY

LEIGH HODGKINSON & CHRIS JEVONS

Farshore

Onesie party,
Onesie party,
Everyone's **invited**!

Onesie party,
Onesie party,
Everyone's excited!

Onesie party,
Onesie party,
What do you want to wear?

Onesie party,
Onesie party,

Tiger . . .

Fish . . .

or **bear?**

Mouse can be a croc,

And Elephant
a cat.

Croc can be a snail,

And Cat
a hairy bat.

Worm wants to
be a butterfly.

Bird wants to
be a moose.

While Panda, Fox and Lion
All want to be a goose!

Onesie party,
Onesie party,
Come on time to **go**!

Onesie party,

Onesie party,

Hurry -
don't be slow!

Onesie party,
Onesie party,
Dancing in a line!

Onesie party,
Onesie party,
Have a **super** time!

Fluff, fur, hoof, tusk,
Scales, beaks, wings.
Snouts, claws, ears, paws
And lots of other things!

What a Onesie Party
It is turning out to be!
How many party animals
In onesies can **YOU** see?

Onesie party,
Onesie party,
This has been a **blast!**

Onesie party,
Onesie party,

Now home to bed and **fast!**

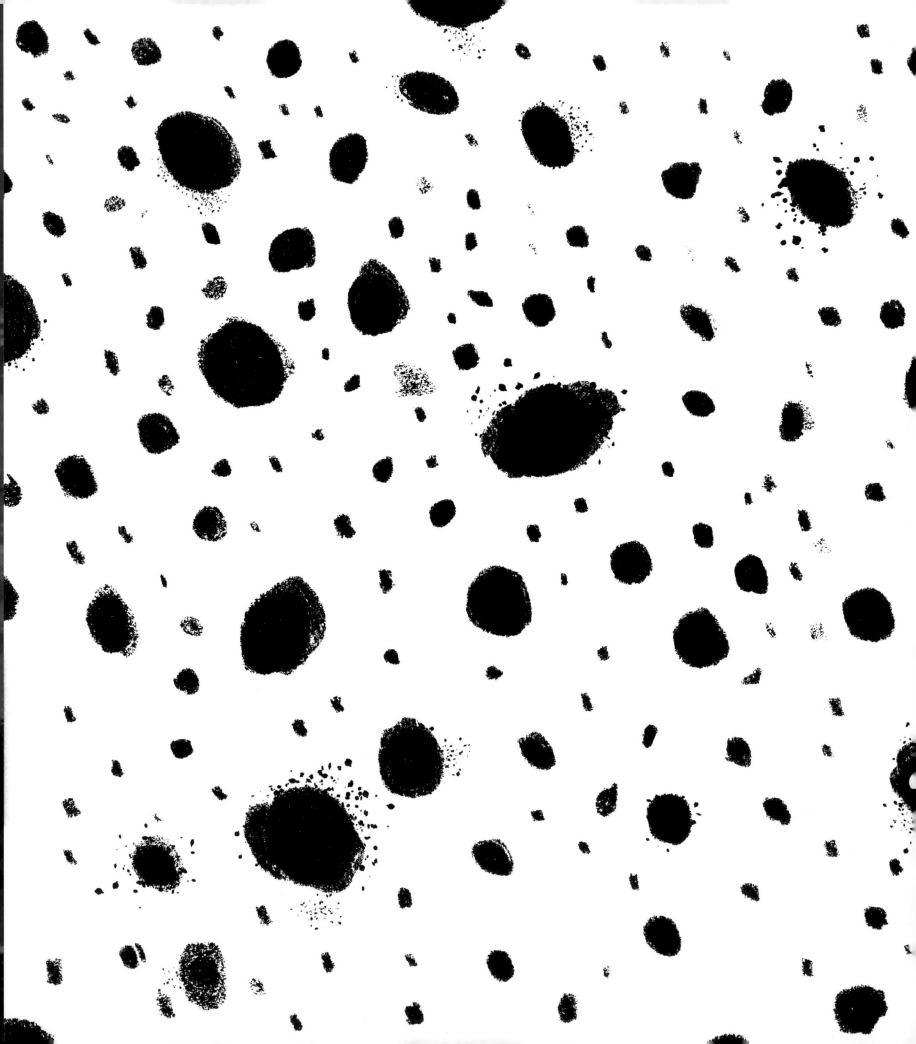